Got Game

FOOTBALL TEAMS BY THE NUMBERS

Nicki Clausen Grace
and Jeff Grace

BLACK RABBIT BOOKS

Bolt is published by Black Rabbit Books
P.O. Box 3263, Mankato, Minnesota, 56002.
www.blackrabbitbooks.com

Jennifer Besel, editor; Michael Sellner, interior and cover designer; Omay Ayres, photo researcher

Library of Congress Cataloging-in-Publication Data
Names: Clausen-Grace, Nicki, author. | Grace, Jeff, 1967- author.
Title: Football Teams by the Numbers / by Nicki Clausen Grace and Jeff Grace.
Description: Mankato, Minnesota : Black Rabbit Books, 2018. | Series: Bolt. Got Game | Includes bibliographical references and index. | Audience: Age 9-12. | Audience: Grade 4 to 6.
Identifiers: LCCN 2016049951 (print) | LCCN 2017005243 (ebook) | ISBN 9781680721461 (library binding) | ISBN 9781680722109 (e-book) | ISBN 9781680724950 (paperback)
Subjects: LCSH: Football teams–United States–History–Juvenile literature. | Football–Records–United States–Juvenile literature.
Classification: LCC GV954 C57 2018 (print) | LCC GV954 (ebook) | DDC 796.332/640973-dc23
LC record available at https://lccn.loc.gov/2016049951

Printed in the United States at CG Book Printers, North Mankato, Minnesota, 56003. 3/17

Image Credits

AP Images: Ben Margot, 1, Back Cover; David J. Phillip, 16; Eric Lars Bakke, 8; Kevin Terrell, 17 (bottom); Paul Abell, 26, 28–29; Ross D. Franklin, 7; Corbis: Unknown, 8–9 (trophy); Getty Images: Doug Pensinger, Cover; Fred Kaplan, 13; Newscom: Andrew Dieb/Icon Sportswire CEY, 4–5; Shutterstock: browndogstudios, 10 (helmet), 26–27 (helmets); Dimec, 24–25 (green silhouettes); EFKS, 3, 18–19 (stadium), 24–25 (stadium); Orgus88, 11 (football); Svyatoslav Aleksandrov, 31; VitaminCo, 7 (footballs), 10 (footballs), 13 (football), 24–25 (footballs), 26–27 (footballs), 32; USA Today Images: Evan Habeeb, 20; Joe Nicholson, 23; Mark J. Rebilas, 17 (top); Matthew Emmons, 14
Every effort has been made to contact copyright holders for material reproduced in this book. Any omissions will be rectified in subsequent printings if notice is given to the publisher.

Contents

CHAPTER 1

Working for the Win

The quarterback throws a pass to a **receiver**. The linemen knock down **defenders**. The receiver races in for the touchdown!

All players on a team must work together. They push the ball down the field and score. Team members who work together win.

CHAPTER 2

Super Bowl Superstars

Teams have to work hard and play well to get to the Super Bowl. Some amazing teams have played in the Super Bowl many times.

The Pittsburgh Steelers are no strangers to the Super Bowl. The team has played the Super Bowl eight times. It won six of those games.

Super Bowl Winning Percentages
83%
San Francisco 49ers
75%
Pittsburgh Steelers
63%
Dallas Cowboys

San Francisco 49ers

The 49ers are close behind the Steelers. This team has five Super Bowl wins. It also holds a Super Bowl record. The 49ers scored the most points in a Super Bowl game.

By the Numbers

9
most appearances
New England Patriots

6 most wins
Pittsburgh Steelers

5
most losses
Denver Broncos

55
most points scored in a game
San Francisco 49ers

4
most Super Bowl losses in a row
Buffalo Bills

4
most Super Bowls played in a row
Buffalo Bills

as of 2016 season

Miami Dolphins

A perfect season doesn't happen very often. In fact, the Dolphins are the only team to have played a perfect season. The team won all its games in the 1972 season. Those wins included the Super Bowl.

Dolphins' Perfect Season

(regular season)

total passing yards
2,235

total rushing yards
2,960

total touchdowns
45

total points scored
385

total points allowed
171

The Cowboys haven't played in the Super Bowl in more than 20 years. But the team is worth more than any other NFL team.

CHAPTER 3

On the Money

For some people, football isn't just about winning. Players, owners, and other people make money from the game.

Teams don't have to be Super Bowl superstars to win big. The Dallas Cowboys are worth more than $4 billion. In 2015 alone, the team earned $700 million.

New England Patriots

The Patriots are worth big money too. The team is worth more than $3 billion.

Fans help teams make money by buying game tickets. The Patriots charge the most for tickets. A regular seat at a Patriots' game costs $130.

special teams players

paid $6,387,500

Money Patriots Spent on Players in 2016

offensive players

paid
$70,165,977

defensive players

paid
$63,502,587

COMPARING AVERAGE SALARIES

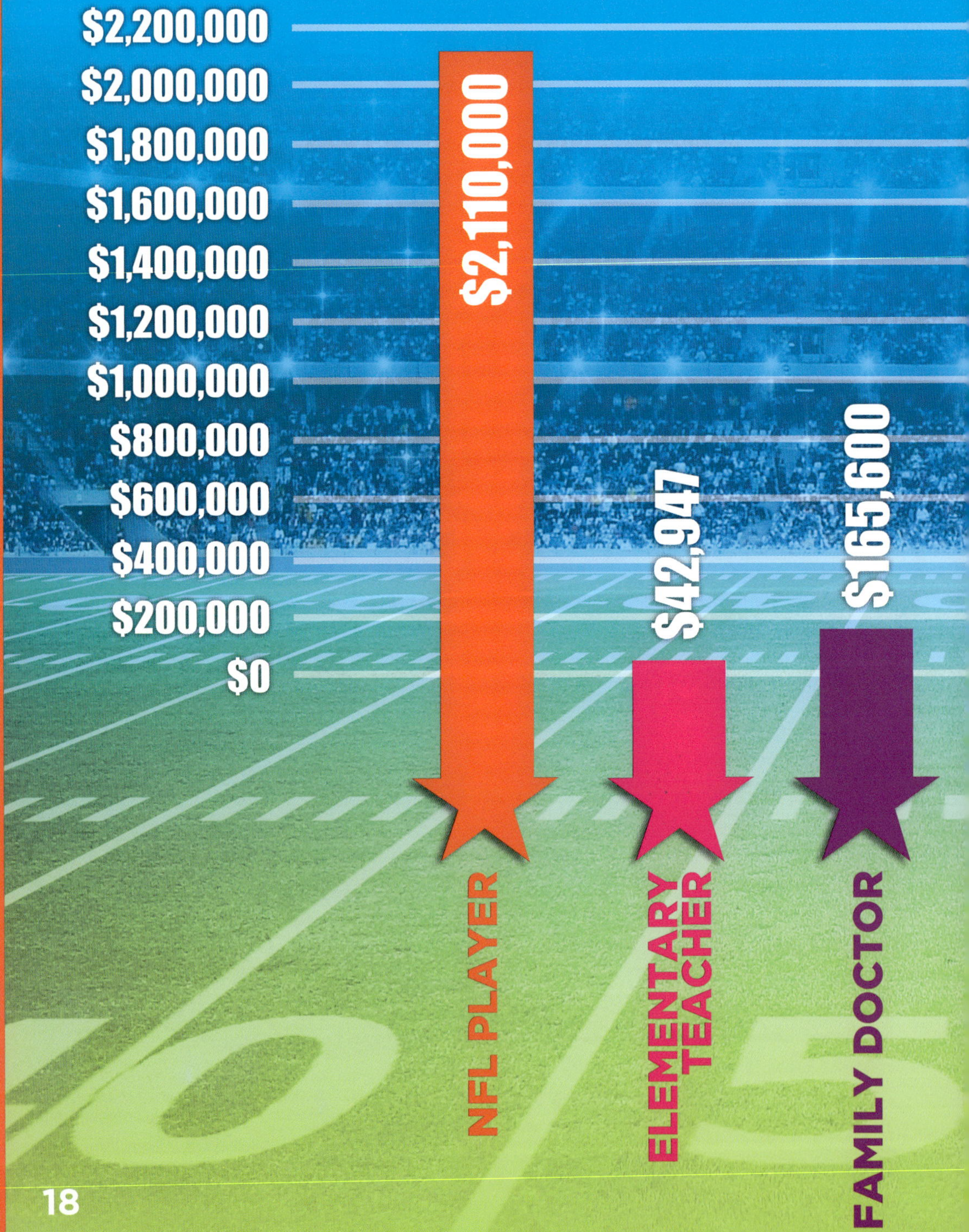

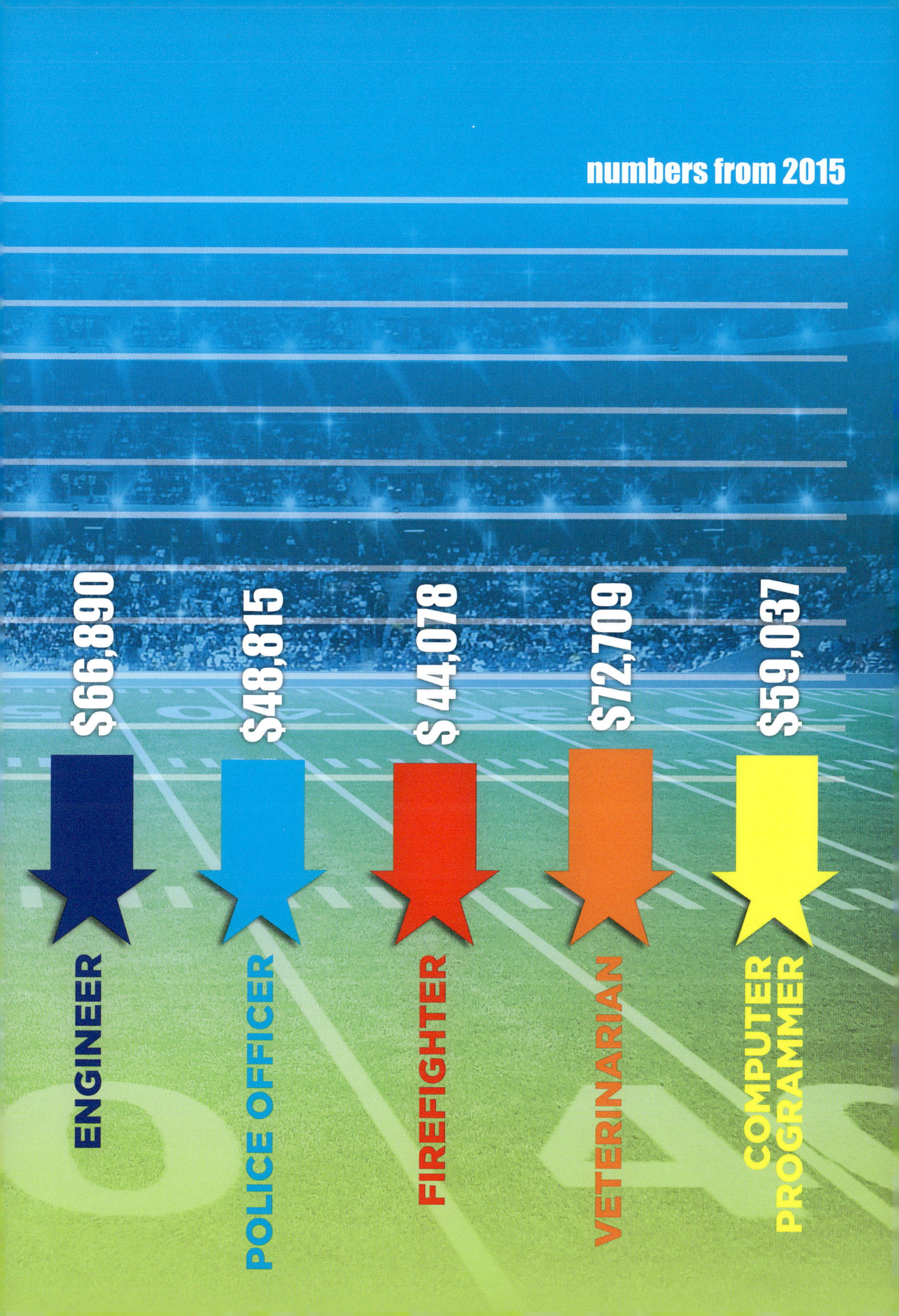
numbers from 2015
$66,890
ENGINEER
$48,815
POLICE OFFICER
$44,078
FIREFIGHTER
$72,709
VETERINARIAN
$59,037
COMPUTER PROGRAMMER

Washington Redskins

It would cost about $2,950,000,000 to buy the Redskins. In 2016, it was the fifth most **valuable** NFL team. The team brought in $447 million in 2015.

The Redskins were purchased for $750 million in 1999.

CHAPTER 4

Every Point Counts

Every football game is really a bunch of math problems. Players and coaches subtract yards for a **first down**. They add up points too.

The 2015 Seattle Seahawks were great at keeping teams from scoring. The team only allowed **opponents** to score about 17 points per game. That **average** was the season's best.

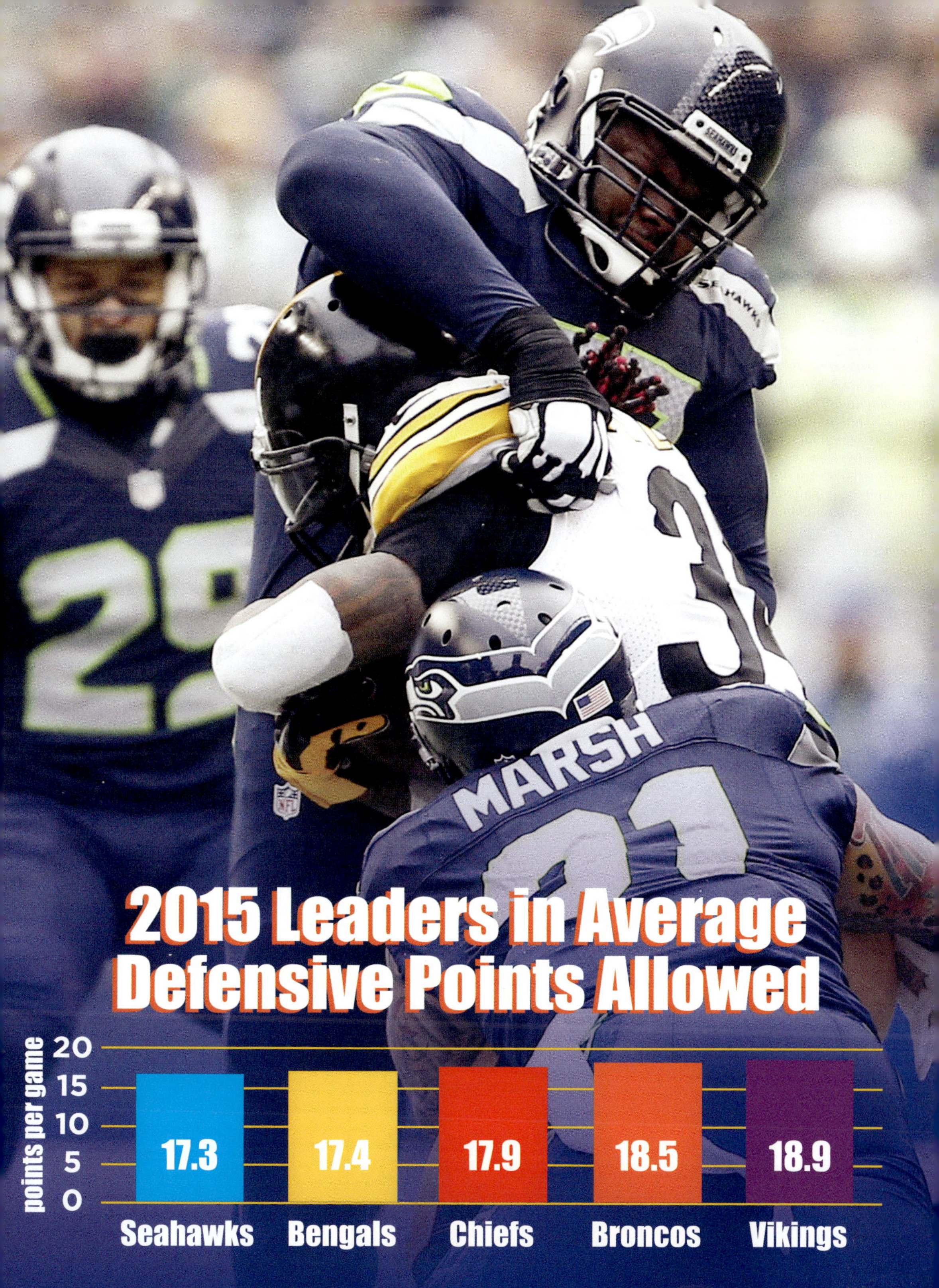
2015 Leaders in Average Defensive Points Allowed
points per game
20
15
10
5
0
17.3
17.4
17.9
18.5
18.9
Seahawks
Bengals
Chiefs
Broncos
Vikings
MARSH
SEAHAWKS

TOP 2016 NFL OFFENSIVE TEAMS
(regular season)

Total Yards

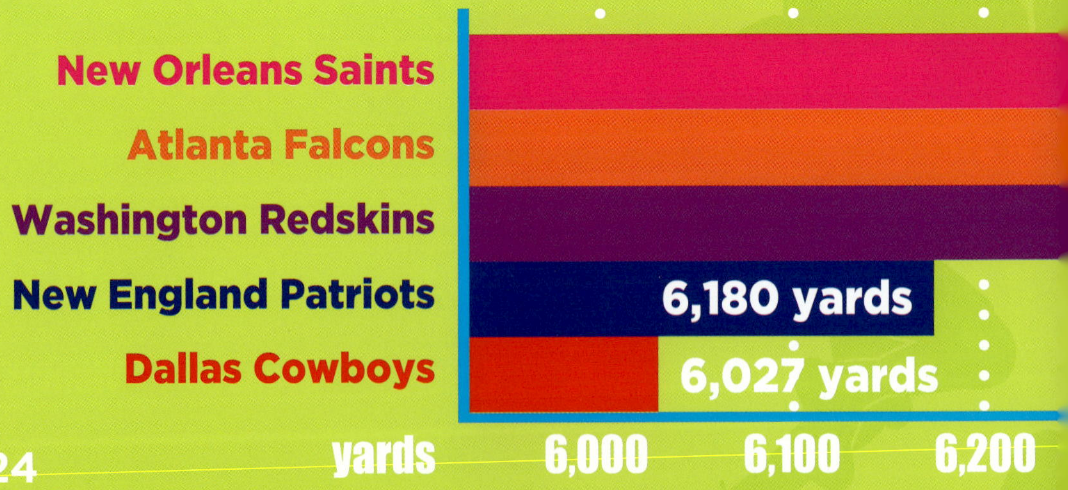

Total Touchdowns

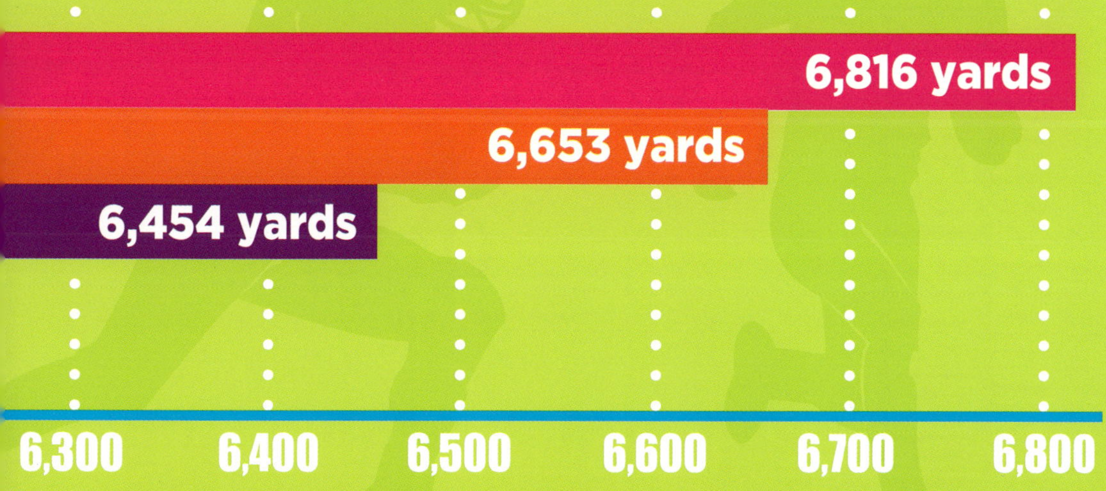

PACKERS' AVERAGE POINTS PER GAME
18.8
2006
23.0

Green Bay Packers

The numbers weren't bad for the Packers in 2016. The team averaged 27.0 points per game. But that wasn't the Packers' best season. In 2011 and 2014 the team led the league in points.

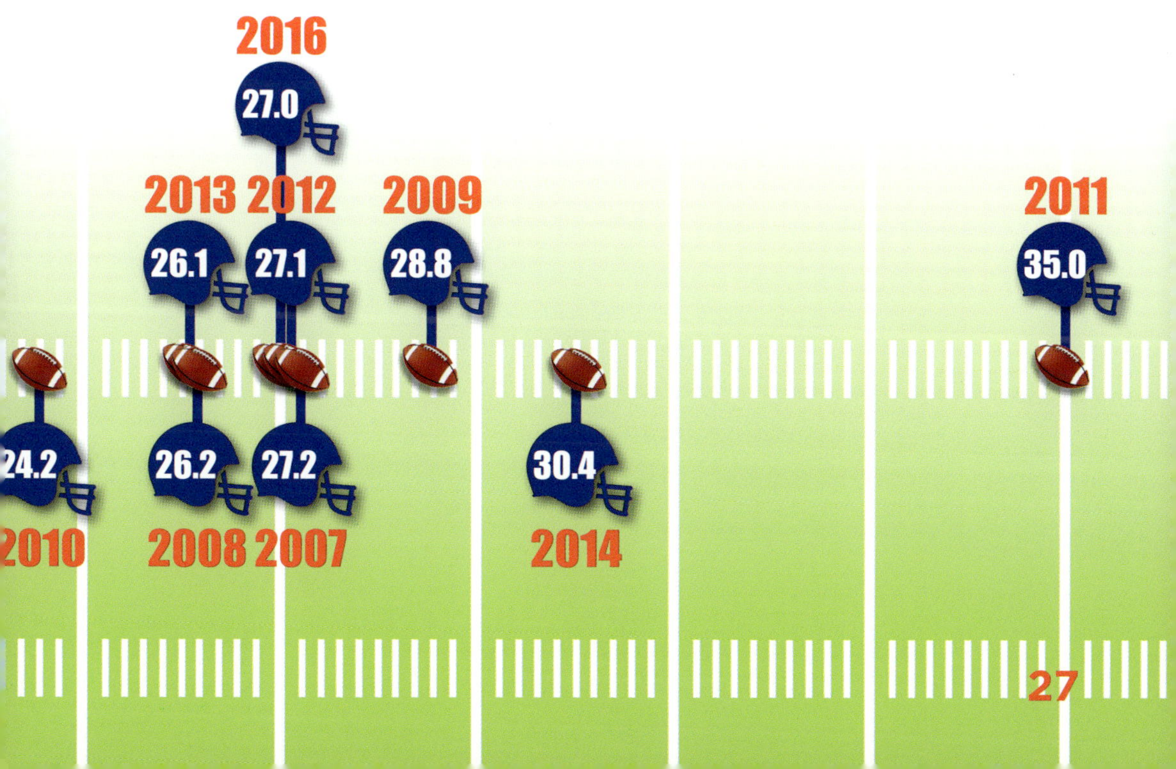

Number Fun

Numbers are a fun part of football. Fans keep score. Teams track their wins and losses. Get excited watching football by the numbers!

BRYANT

GLOSSARY

average (AHV-rij)—a number that is calculated by adding quantities together and then dividing the total by the number of quantities

defender (de-FEN-dur)—a player who works to stop the other team from scoring

first down (FURST DAHWN)—the first of a series of four plays in which the team must gain 10 yards to keep the ball

offensive (oh-FEN-siv)—relating to the attempt to score in a game

opponent (uh-POH-nunt)—a person, team, or group that is competing against another

receiver (reh-SEE-vur)—a football player who catches passes thrown by the quarterback

rushing (RUSH-ing)—moving the football toward the goal by using running plays

valuable (VAL-yoo-bul)—worth a lot of money

LEARN MORE

BOOKS

Anastasio, Dina. *What Is the Super Bowl?* What Was…? New York: Grosset & Dunlap, an imprint of Penguin Random House, 2015.

Cosson, M. J. *Superstars of the Green Bay Packers.* Pro Sports Superstars. Mankato, MN: Amicus, 2014.

Gilbert, Sara. *The Story of the Washington Redskins.* NFL Today. Mankato, MN: Creative Education, 2014.

WEBSITES

Football: List of NFL Teams
www.ducksters.com/sports/list_of_nfl_teams.php

NFL RUSH
www.nflrush.com

NFL Teams
www.nfl.com/teams

INDEX